DIARY OF AN ICE PRINCESS

Frost Friends Forever

For Neave, Anne Louise,
and Hudspeth

ISBN 978-1-338-35397-6

10 9 8 7 6 5 4 3 2 19 20 21 22 23

Printed in the U.S.A. 23

First printing 2019

Book design by Yaffa Jaskoll

Frost Friends Forever

by

Christina Soontornvat

Illustrations by

Barbara Szepesi Szucs

SCHOLASTIC INC.

1

Bring on the Break

WEDNESDAY

Dear Diary,

This weekend is the start of Hilltop Science and Arts Academy's winter break, and I have to say I'm pretty excited.

Don't get me wrong, I love school. What's not to love?

My best friend, Claudia, sits next to me in class. ✓

Ms. Collier is the coolest teacher ever. ✓

I get to be a regular kid, and no one knows I'm actually a princess. ✓

But even though school is awesome, I'm looking forward to having no homework for a little while. Ms. Collier did give us one assignment, but it actually sounds fun.

"Class, I want you all to keep a Science Observation Notebook over the break," she told us this morning. "Whenever you notice science in action, write it down in your notebook. It can be anything we've learned about in class: animals, moving objects, weather . . ."

Claudia nudged me. "Speaking of weather, when are you going to make it snow?" she whispered. "I haven't *observed* a single snowflake yet."

"Very funny," I whispered back. "You know I can't use my powers at school."

This year I learned that I'm a Winterheart, which means that I have magic powers over ice and snow. Most of my family members are Windtamers (they can control the wind and weather).

It's great to finally know why my magic is always icy, especially because it has helped me keep my powers under

control. I can't let anyone at school know about my royal status or my magic (except for Claudia, of course). The only downside is that I can't go out on the playground right now and make a blizzard! Claudia's right—we could use a little winter fun around here.

But the number one reason I'm excited for the break is that Claudia and I have Big Plans. Big Sleepover Plans.

I can't wait, Diary. Bring on the winter!

2

The Bold and the Brave

THURSDAY

So much for Big Plans, Diary.

Today at lunch, Claudia gave me the worst news ever.

"You can't stay at my house over the break," she said. "*I'm* not even staying at my house over the break."

I nearly choked on my carrot stick. "Why not?"

"My big brother is starting at college, and my parents have to help him move in. They're making me come with them."

Claudia's family are the only Groundlings who know my family's big royal secret. I love them almost as much as my own family. How could they do this to me?

"But what about our observation homework for Ms. Collier?" I asked.

"The only thing I'll be observing is the

CLAUDIA'S FAMILY

backseat of the car. Our road trip is going to take ten hours. Each way!"

Poor Claudia. Poor me! Sleepovers at her house are the best thing on earth (or in the sky). We use the trampoline, eat pizza, and watch all the movies we want!

I could almost smell the pancakes and

sausage Claudia's mom always cooks us for breakfast. Not only were we not going to have any sleepovers, but I wasn't even going to have a friend to play with during the break!

Diary, I had to be bold. I had to take matters into my own hands.

"Don't go on that boring road trip with your family!" I blurted out. "Come sleep over at my house instead."

Claudia leaned in and gave me a look. It was her *have-you-lost-your-marbles?* look. "Your *house*?"

I knew what she meant. We don't live in a house. We live in a palace in the clouds. And I have never had a friend sleep over before. But there has to be a first time for everything.

"You think your mom will let you?" I asked.

Claudia chewed her sandwich for a long time. "Possibly. But we're going to need a new Routine of Persuasion."

3

The Ultimate Routine

FRIDAY

Whenever Claudia and I want our parents to agree to something big, we don't just ask for it.

We perform the Routine of Persuasion.

Our routine is a mix of dance, acrobatics, jokes, and begging. It's much harder for our parents to say no to us when we dazzle them.

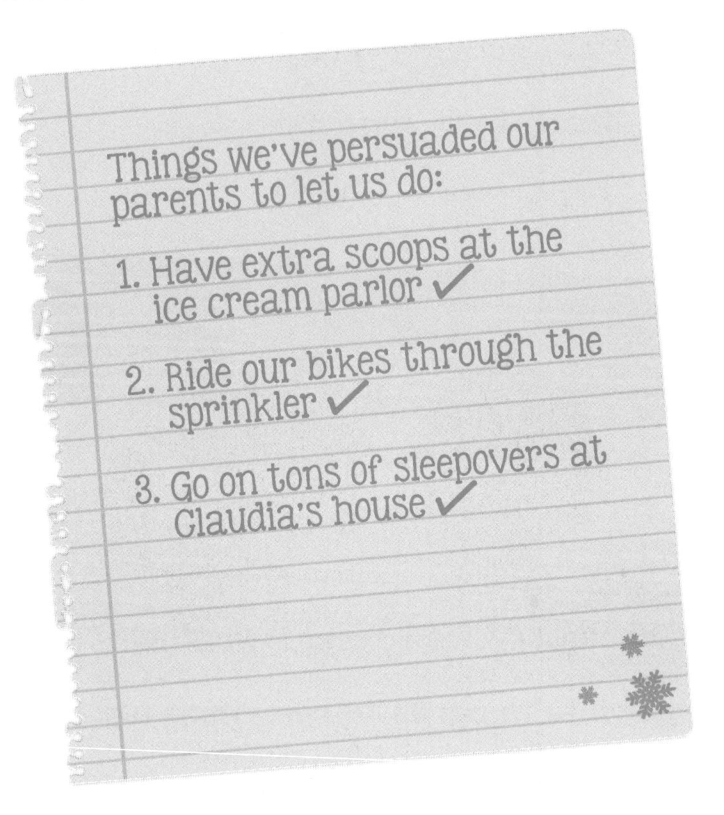

But getting them to agree to a cloud palace sleepover means that our routine needs a secret weapon.

Today was the last day of school before winter break started.

"You ready?" asked Claudia as soon as the end-of-school bell rang.

"I was born ready," I said.

(I had actually finished getting ready a few minutes before, but who's counting?)

Claudia's mom was waiting with my dad and Gusty in the pickup area. Before they could even ask, "How was your day?" we launched into the best, most persuasive routine of our lives.

And then we brought in our secret weapon:

After we were done, Dad laughed. "We'd love to have Claudia sleep over anytime! As long as her mom says it's okay, of course."

Claudia's mom gave her a look. It was her *I'm-thinking-about-it* look. "All right," she said. "I was worried about you being bored on the road trip anyway. You can go."

Oh, Diary! I am going to have my first sleepover at my own house!

4

Preparing for Perfection

SATURDAY

Three nights. That's how long Claudia is going to stay with us while her parents drive her brother to college.

Three whole, amazing nights!

Dad is bringing her up in the plane later this evening, which means I have just a few hours to get everything ready for the perfect sleepover.

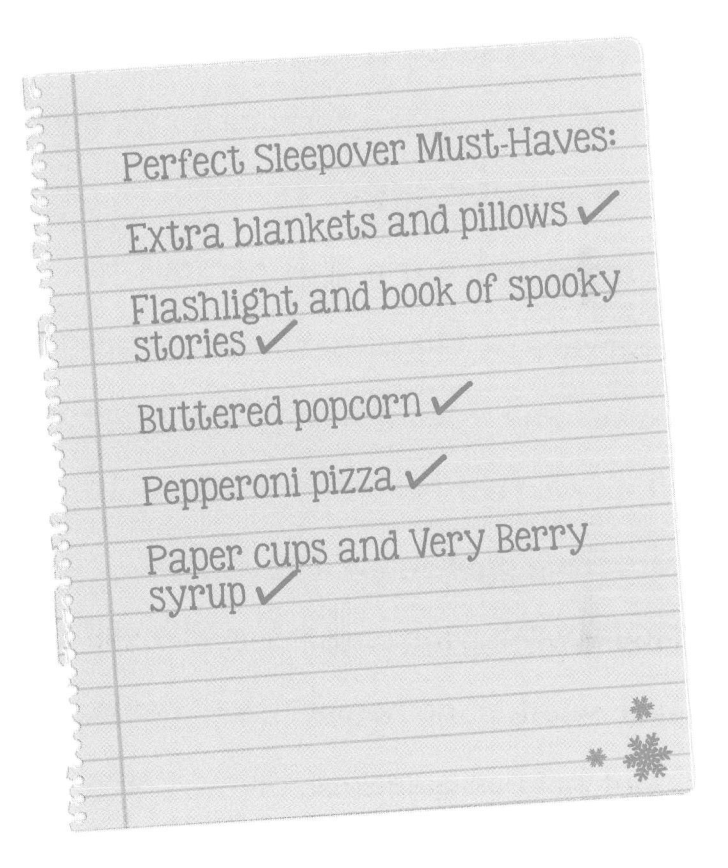
Perfect Sleepover Must-Haves:

Extra blankets and pillows ✓

Flashlight and book of spooky stories ✓

Buttered popcorn ✓

Pepperoni pizza ✓

Paper cups and Very Berry syrup ✓

Claudia loves snow cones, and with my powers I'm like a snow cone factory.

I begged Mom to get a trampoline, but of course she said no. Instead I'm planning to use my powers to make a big drift of snow on the terrace so we can have snowball fights.

I'm excited, but a little nervous too. Sleepovers at Claudia's house are always so awesome. I want everything to be just as perfect here at our house. If everything goes according to plan, Claudia will have so much fun she will never want to go home!

But hold on a second, Diary. I smell something.

It smells like . . . boiled root vegetables.

Oh no. Oh no, no, no, no.

That can mean only one thing.

Great-Aunt Eastia is here.

5

An Unexpected Guest

Ugh, Diary, I just got back from talking to Mom downstairs.

As soon as I smelled the vegetables, I raced to her office and shut the door quietly behind me.

"Mom! What is Great-Aunt Eastia doing here?" I whispered.

"I told you before," Mom said. "She's staying with us for a few weeks."

She did *not* tell me that.

(Okay, maybe she did and I forgot. But that's beside the point.)

"Mom, she can't stay here. She's going to ruin my sleepover!"

Mom's eyebrows pinched together, which meant she was feeling very disappointed in me.

"Lina, I am very disappointed in you. That is a selfish thing to say. You know how much Aunt Eastia loves you."

I know that Great-Aunt Eastia loves me. And I love her too, I really do. She tells wonderful stories, and she

taught me how to play the piano. But she is also old and strict, and she is always telling me to act more like a princess.

Great-Aunt Eastia grew up in a different time, when princesses were supposed to be—well, princess-like. But I can't argue with her about it because that would be rude. And princesses are never rude to their elders.

Great-Aunt Eastia's Princess Don'ts:

Princesses don't slouch. ✓

Princesses don't chew gum. ✓

Princesses don't roll on the ground with their dogs. ✓

Princesses don't freeze the stair railing so they can slide all the way down. ✓

Mom patted my arm. "It's going to be fine, sweetie. You won't even notice she's here. Just be respectful . . ."

"Of course, Mom."

". . . and mind your manners . . ."

"Of course, Mom."

". . . and remember, no winter magic while she's here."

"What?!"

"The cold makes her joints hurt," Mom said. "We're going to keep things as comfortable as possible while she's our guest."

Great-Aunt Eastia is a Windtamer, just like my mom and Granddad. But now that she's older, she hates the cold and

almost always wears a thick coat, even inside.

There went my plans for snow cones and ice sculpture competitions with Claudia. Just then there was a tap at the door and Great-Aunt Eastia came in.

I bowed to her, and then she hugged me tight. "My favorite great-niece!" she said. "I heard you are doing so well in school! I'm very proud of you. But, Lina, what have I told you? Stand up straight. And when was the last time you brushed

your hair? Don't forget—you are a princess!"

Oh, Diary. I would love to forget it for just once in my life. But no one will let me!

6

Turnip Troubles

I waited in the front hall of the palace for ages, checking and rechecking to see when Claudia would arrive. Finally I heard the *zhum!* of Dad's plane. She was here!

Gusty and I threw open the front doors, and Claudia bounded across the clouds to me. We were so excited that we did our super-secret best-friend dance twice.

"This cloud castle is unbelievable," said Claudia, looking around. "Ms. Collier said that clouds are just made out of dust and water droplets."

"And magic," I said. "I mean, *our* clouds are made of magic. Otherwise we'd all be dropping out of the sky right now."

Mom gave Claudia a big hug. "We're so glad you're here! Lina, why don't you take Claudia up to your room and help her settle in."

I led the way upstairs to my bedroom. I don't know why, Diary, but I felt

nervous! I've never had a friend visit my room before today. At least I had cleaned it up (which means I shoved everything under my bed and into my closet).

I showed Claudia the paper cups and syrup. "These are for later."

Her eyes lit up. "Very Berry? Now this is the best sleepover ever."

We celebrated by jumping on the bed. I was feeling great! Until we went down to dinner.

I smelled food. It didn't smell like double pepperoni.

"Dad," I whispered. "Where's the pizza?"

"Honey, we can have pizza another night. Great-Aunt Eastia wanted to make dinner tonight."

My great-aunt came into the dining room, followed by waiters carrying big, steaming soup bowls.

"I made your favorite, Lina," she said. "My special winter stew."

I usually like it fine, but it is definitely *not* pizza. I watched Claudia nervously.

She leaned over her bowl and took a slow sip. "*Mmm*, that's very delicious, Ms. Eastia."

Great-Aunt Eastia beamed. "Thank you, my dear. Lina, I like your friend already. And do you see the way she holds her spoon? No splashing. Perhaps you could learn something from her."

I sat up super straight and sipped my soup with no splashes (okay, maybe just a couple splashes. Small ones).

GREAT-AUNT EASTIA'S WINTER STEW:

- Purple turnips
- White turnips
- Pink turnips
- Pork bones
- More turnips

Gusty got his own bowl of stew.

At least someone in the room made a bigger mess than I did.

7

Checkmate

Diary, I'm writing this from my bed. It's only nine o'clock, and Claudia is already asleep, which should tell you how the rest of the night went.

After dinner we went into the parlor room. Great-Aunt Eastia sat by the

fireplace with Mom and Dad while Claudia and I played games.

"Checkmate!" said Claudia (for the third time). "Want to play again?"

I slumped in my chair. If we were a normal family, we would have been watching a movie. But we don't have any movies. We don't even have a television!

Turnip soup and chess? This wasn't the fun sleepover I imagined at all. Then I had a brilliant idea.

"Mom, Dad, we've got to go do our homework," I said.

"Right now?" Mom asked.

"Never too early to start. Right, Claudia?" I gave her my *please-go-along-with-it* look.

Claudia got the hint. "Yup. The early bird gets the—er, good grades?"

"Such studious young girls," said Great-Aunt Eastia.

We said our good nights, and I pulled Claudia out into the hallway.

"You don't seriously want to do homework right now, do you?" Claudia whispered.

"Of course I do! Ms. Collier said we were supposed to observe science in action. I think we should observe one of the forces we learned about in class."

Claudia gave me her *what-are-you-up-to?* look. "Is this going to involve *ice?*"

I smiled really, really big. "Trust me, this will be way better than sitting in that boring old parlor room."

"It wasn't boring," said Claudia, but I knew she was just trying to be nice.

I took her hand and led her down the hall. "Come on. This is in the name of science!"

8

Frictionless Fun

Yes, Diary, I know.

I'm not supposed to use my powers while Great-Aunt Eastia is visiting. But we were in the ballroom, which is all the way at the other end of the castle, so I figured she would never know.

Ms. Collier taught us that when two objects rub against each other, they cause friction. Like when you rub your hands together to warm them up. Or when you push a chair across the room. Or when you give your dog a really good backrub.

When something slides across a surface, the force of friction will slow it down. But if the surface is really smooth and slippery—like, ahem, *ice*—friction is lower, and that makes for epic sliding.

I checked one more time that the ballroom doors were closed. Then I turned to Claudia. "Are you ready, Observation Partner?"

Claudia tapped her pencil on her notebook. "Ready to observe!"

I held up my hands and took a deep breath. Until a few months ago, my winter magic would slip out and do wacky things. But ever since I learned that I'm a Winterheart, I've been much better at controlling my powers. Even so, I didn't want anyone to know what we were doing, so I tried to keep things as chill as possible.

Luckily ice is as chill as it gets.

I waved my hands in front of me and let my breath out slowly. A thin layer of

ice coated the floor. I laid down another layer, and another, until the ice was thick and smooth.

Claudia grinned. "Okay, let's see some low friction in action!"

I grabbed a cushion off one of the ballroom chairs, took a running start, and slid on my belly all the way across the room! "*Wheeeeeeee!*"

"Not bad," Claudia said. "But I think my cushion will slide even farther. Please stand back—in the name of science!"

We observed every cushion in the room.

After a little while, we started

observing each other doing awesome tricks, like a 360-degree spin.

I landed my spin gracefully (okay, I slammed into the wall, but with *pizzazz*). "Claudia, it's your turn again! Claudia?"

Claudia had a petrified look on her face as she pointed behind me.

I turned around and saw Great-Aunt Eastia with her hands on her hips.

Gosh, Diary, who knew someone could glare with disapproval and shiver at the same time?

9

A Scolding Fit for a Princess

Great-Aunt Eastia might seem like a sweet, older lady, but she is also a powerful member of the Windtamer royal family. In that moment, she looked like a very *angry* member of the royal family. With a snap of her fingers, a hot, dry wind rolled through the room, melting the ice and evaporating it.

I may have trembled, just a little bit.

"Lina, this behavior is *not* fit for a young princess," she said.

"I'm sorry, we were just–"

"This is a palace, not a circus. Not only that, but when I went to check on you I found bottles of syrup in your room. Sugary syrup will rot your teeth. And it attracts ants!"

Ants? How are ants going to get up here, Diary? We live on a cloud!

Great-Aunt Eastia pulled her coat tighter. "You also promised your mother that you wouldn't use your winter magic while I'm here."

"We were just trying to have some fun."

My great-aunt's expression softened. "Lina, do you understand what it means to be a princess?"

"Yes," I said with a small sigh. "Stand up straight. Mind my manners."

Great-Aunt Eastia shook her head. "It means that you act honorably. It means that you think about other people, not just about yourself. It means you keep your promises."

I didn't know what to say, so I just stared down at my feet.

"You and Claudia will go straight to bed," said Great-Aunt Eastia. "Or else I will have to have a discussion with your parents."

We couldn't argue with that. Claudia and I trudged upstairs. Claudia seemed really sad, Diary. I think she is disappointed. And who could blame her?

No pizza, no movies, no fun of any kind. And now we can't even have snow cones. This sleepover is a complete disaster.

But I'm not going to give up just because my old-fashioned great-aunt wants me to act "like a princess." I have to do something.

Diary, tomorrow morning Operation Sleepover goes into full effect.

10

Operation Sleepover Begins

SUNDAY

This is how it all happened.

This morning, I woke Claudia up early.

She is not a morning person.

"Listen, do you want to see the most amazing winter magic of your entire life?"

Claudia sat up. "But what about Great-Aunt Eastia? After last night, you definitely can't use your powers inside."

"I'm not talking about using them inside the castle. I'm talking about using them on the ground. My dad is taking the plane down today to go grocery shopping. He parks the plane very close to these big hills that are perfect for sledding—with a little snowy help from me, of course."

Claudia's eyes lit up. I explained my plan to her:

The plan:

1. We sneak onto Dad's plane. ✓
2. While he runs errands, we run over to the hills. ✓
3. Snow! Sledding! Winter magic fun! ✓
4. We sneak back onto the plane. ✓
5. No one is the wiser! ✓

"Easy, right?" I said.

Claudia didn't look convinced. "Are you sure that we won't get in trouble?"

"I'm sure. I go on shopping trips with my dad all the time, so I know exactly how long it takes him. Come on, it's way better than staying in this boring old castle."

"It would be nice to be on the ground for a little while . . ."

"And I promise this will be the best sledding of your entire life! Please, Claudia? Don't make me do a routine to win you over!"

Claudia laughed. "You can't do a routine without my help, anyway, silly. Okay. Let's do it."

11

Take to the Skies

Claudia and I snuck over to the hangar where Dad keeps his plane. We hid behind a big bin of spare tires, waiting for the perfect moment to sneak on board.

"You brought your backpack?" I whispered.

Claudia nodded. "I packed some supplies, just in case. You know, snacks and stuff like that."

"It looks pretty lumpy for just snacks," I said.

"Trust me, you are going to be glad that I brought this."

Just then, my dad came into the hangar and swung his jacket and goggles up into his plane, then went back into the storeroom.

"Okay," I whispered to Claudia. "Now's our chance!"

We hurried over to the plane. Silently we hopped into the backseat and covered ourselves up with blankets. I smiled. This was really going to work!

That's when I heard a whimpering sound coming from outside the plane.

Gusty!

I'd forgotten to close him in my room.

He was going to ruin everything!

I sat up and leaned out over the plane. "Gusty, go on! Get back inside!" I whispered. He stayed put.

That dog. He never listens to me.

"Okay, get up here, but you have to be quiet!"

Gusty leaped into my arms, and I pulled him in beside me just as my dad came back around the corner.

I held my breath. Claudia held her breath. Gusty can't hold his breath. It smells like doggie chow. But at least he was quiet.

My dad started the engine, and we were off!

12

The Perfect Hill

We didn't exactly have the most comfortable ride to Earth. There must have been some really thick clouds because the ride was bumpier than usual. I was glad when Dad finally coasted down to the airfield.

We waited until we were sure he was gone and then popped our heads up. We climbed down out of the plane, with Gusty at our heels. He loves coming down to the ground!

"See? Nothing to it!" I told Claudia.

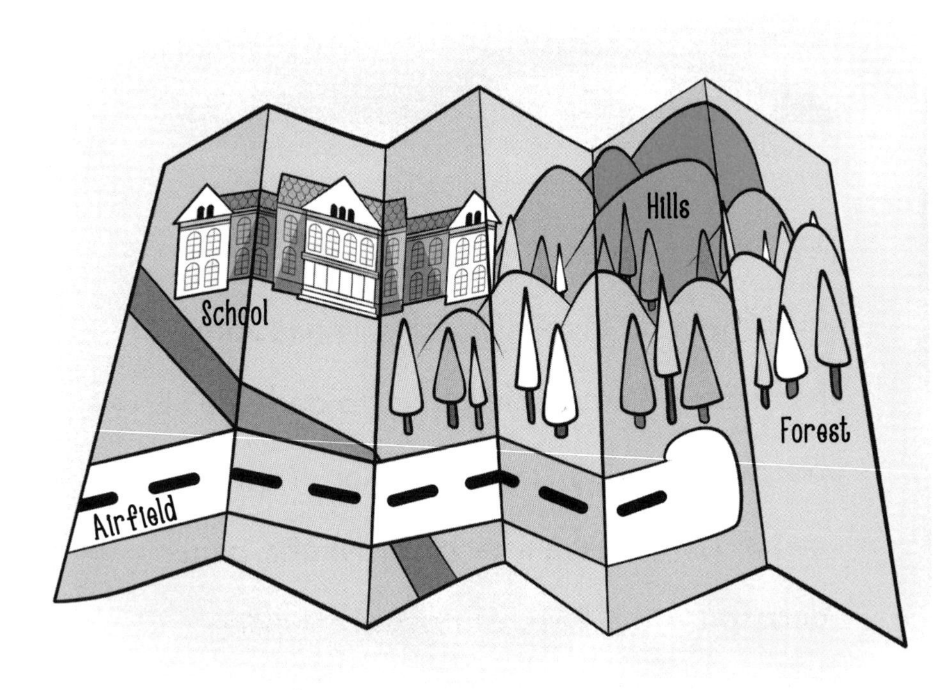

We trekked to the hill through the trees, which hid us pretty well from the airfield. The air felt chilly, but not freezing cold. The perfect sledding weather.

I breathed deep. It felt so good to be away from the palace. No one here would tell me to act like a princess. No one would tell me to stop trying to have fun.

Claudia grabbed my arm. She looked nervous. "We're only going to be here for a little while, right?"

I nodded. "We'll be back on the plane before my dad even finishes checking out at the grocery store."

"All right, then," Claudia said. "Let it snow!"

I held out my arms. A tingly, excited feeling ran up and down my spine.

Diary, it was time to snow big, or go home.

13

How Snow Can You Go?

The tingly feeling ran down my arms, through my hands, and into my fingertips. I took a big, deep breath. The air smelled crisp and frosty. I could sense every drop of moisture in the air turning into tiny crystals of ice.

Big, fluffy flakes of snow began drifting down all around us.

Claudia opened her mouth and held out her tongue.

"Good?" I asked.

"Just needs a little Very Berry syrup!"

I laughed and waved my fingers like a conductor in front of an orchestra. The snow fell harder. I swirled my arms and the snow drifted and banked, and soon the entire hill was covered in a thick blanket of white snow.

Claudia started rummaging in her backpack.

"Snacks already?" I asked.

"Not snacks. This!" She pulled out a giant metal mixing bowl. She must have found it in the palace kitchen. Was Claudia going to make snow cookies?

She put the bowl on the top of the hill and sat in it. "See ya at the bottom!"

Off she went swooshing down the hill!

I couldn't believe it—it was way better than any sled I'd ever seen! And it spun around while it went down, which looked even more fun!

As soon as I'd made enough snow, I formed my own bowl out of ice and joined her. Diary, it was beyond wonderful.

This was what I had in mind for the perfect winter break with my best friend. Way better than turnip soup and chess. Gusty loved it almost as much as me!

When we got tired, I made an ice bench. We sat on the blanket we brought from the airplane and shared the snacks that Claudia had packed.

I could have stayed out all day, but I knew the fun couldn't last forever. It was time to get back to the plane. We packed everything up and started back up the hill.

"Hey, Lina," said Claudia, huffing and puffing. "You can turn off the snow now, don't you think?"

"What? I did turn it off."

Claudia stopped. "Are you sure?"

"Yes, I'm sure! I'm not using my powers."

"Then what is that?" She pointed to the horizon behind us. Diary, I looked up, and my stomach flipped.

Coming straight toward us was an actual, giant, genuine blizzard.

14

Lost

"We've got to get back to the plane!" I shouted. "Let's go!"

We held hands and ran as fast as we could. But the blizzard was coming in quick. A cold wind gusted across the top of the hill and picked up the snow on the ground, swirling it all around us and

blocking our view. I got nervous that we would lose Gusty, so I picked him up in my arms.

"I think the plane is this way!" shouted Claudia.

"Are you sure? I thought it was that way!"

There was so much snow that we could barely see a few feet in front of us.

"Make it stop, Lina!" Claudia cried.

"I can't!" I shouted back. "I can make snow, but I don't know how to take it away!"

"I feel like we should have reached the plane by now," Claudia said. "What if your dad flies back without us?"

"He won't be able to take off in the storm. He'll wait in the plane until it passes."

At least I hoped he would.

We walked and walked, and the snow

swirled harder all around us. I was getting a bad feeling. I didn't want to say it out loud, but I knew it.

We were lost.

I remembered Mom telling me that if I ever got lost I should stay in one place so I didn't get even more lost. And Dad had once told me that the most important part of survival is having a good shelter.

I raised my hands and formed the whirling snow into a fort with thick walls and a roof. We all crawled in together.

Even though it was still daytime, the storm had made the sky very dark.

I set Gusty down in between us and he whimpered.

"We're going to be okay, right?" Claudia asked.

Diary, I had no idea how to answer her.

15

Some Very Important Observations

Have you ever felt low, Diary? Like really, really awful? Well, take that feeling and multiply it by four thousand, and that's how bad I felt.

What were Mom and Dad going to say? What was Great-Aunt Eastia going to say? She'd probably say I wasn't acting like a princess.

And you know what, Diary? She would be right.

Why I felt really, really awful:

I had snuck away from home. ✓

I had gotten us lost. ✓

I had put my best friend and my dog in danger. ✓

If we ever got out of there, I was going to be in the worst trouble of my life. ✓

If being a princess meant thinking about others and keeping promises, then I was definitely not one. I had made a huge mistake. Okay, a bunch of huge mistakes. I couldn't change any of that.

The only thing I could change was how I acted in that moment.

I decided to start with an apology.

"Claudia, I am so sorry about all this. I talked you into coming down to the ground, and that was wrong. I'm the reason we're lost."

Claudia gave me a look. It was her *yes-this-is-definitely-your-fault* look.

"I just wanted us to have fun," I said.

"The way we do at sleepovers at your house."

"But we *were* having fun," said Claudia. "We always have fun together, no matter what we do."

"Are you kidding? Turnip soup and chess isn't fun compared to trampolines and movies!"

"I don't care about any of that. If I was acting funny, it wasn't because I was bored. It was because I missed my family."

"Wait–what?"

Claudia nodded. "I guess I didn't realize how much I would miss them. Being up in the clouds made them seem

even farther away. I should have explained to you how I was feeling. It's not all your fault, Lina."

Oh, Diary, what a mix-up. Claudia wasn't bored. She was homesick!

I put my hand over hers. "We are

going to get out of this storm. If we put our heads together, we'll find a way. We always do."

Claudia gave me a look. It was her *now-you're-talking* look.

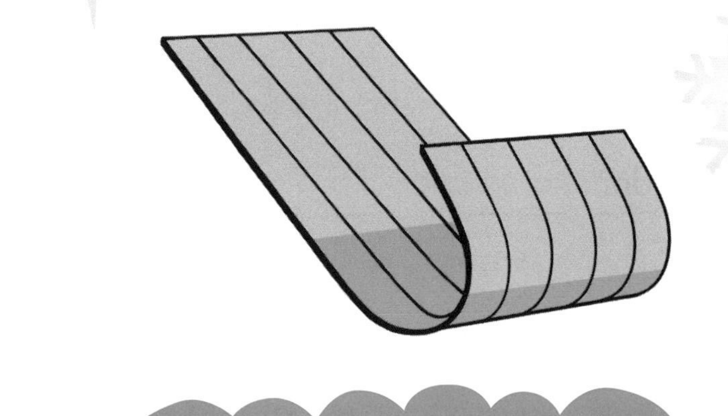

16

Two Heads Are Better

When Claudia is serious about something, her forehead wrinkles up. Right then, she had four wrinkles. That meant she was really serious.

"Okay, we need to take stock of our situation," she said. "We're lost in a blizzard and nobody knows where we are."

I wasn't sure if hearing that out loud made me feel better or worse.

But Claudia smiled. "That's it! Nobody knows where we are, and that's our biggest problem. We might not be able to find our way out of the blizzard, but if we could make a signal, then someone could come find us."

I turned to Gusty. "Give me your biggest howl, buddy."

Gusty howled. It was more like a yippy squeal. It definitely couldn't be heard over the roaring wind.

"I don't suppose you brought a megaphone in your backpack?" I asked.

She shook her head. "But let's see what I do have." Claudia dumped her backpack onto the snow.

We both sighed. It didn't look very promising. Claudia flicked on a key-chain flashlight.

"Definitely not powerful enough to shine through the storm," she said. "But it does look pretty on the snow."

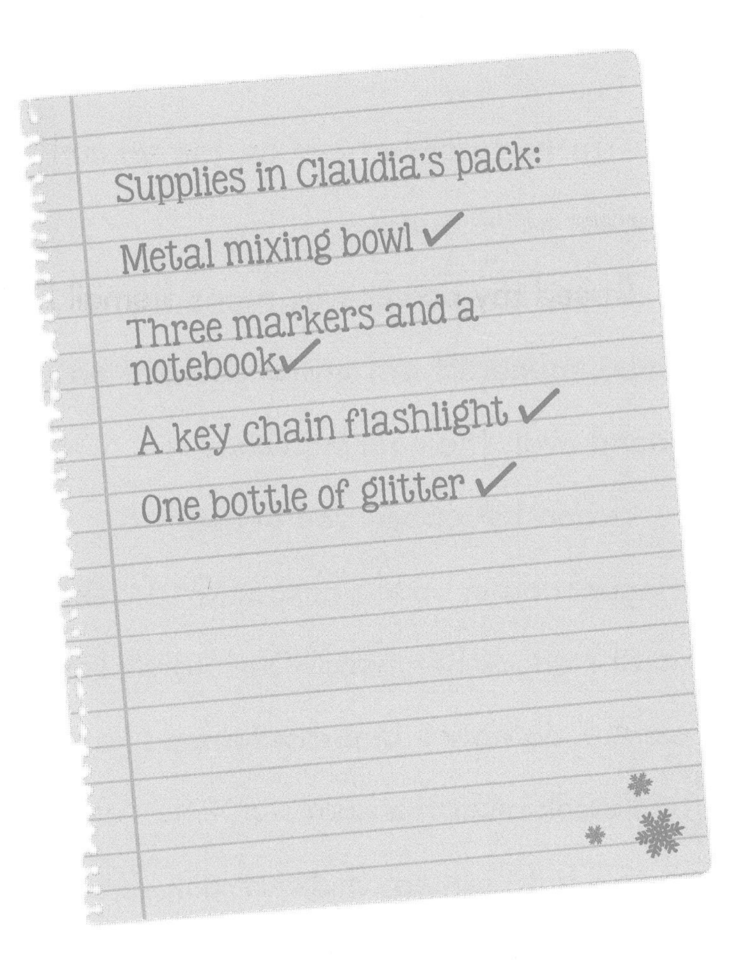
Supplies in Claudia's pack:
Metal mixing bowl ✓
Three markers and a notebook ✓
A key chain flashlight ✓
One bottle of glitter ✓

Suddenly that gave me a wild idea.

"Claudia, that's it! We could use snow or ice to transmit the light. If we do it just right, we could make something big enough to be seen through the storm! Watch . . ."

I used my powers to form a small ball of ice in my hand. I shined the flashlight on the ball. The entire sphere lit up with a pretty red glow.

"That's perfect!" Claudia cried. "We need that, but bigger. Way bigger! Hand me the notebook and markers."

Claudia sketched out her idea for a Super Ice Distress Signaler.

"What's the glitter for?" I asked.

Claudia shrugged. "Everything's better with glitter. Now let's get outside and make this thing!"

MAGIC ICE COLUMN
GLITTER
LINA
CLAUDIA
MIXING BOWL
FLASHLIGHT

17

A Flash of Brilliance

I have never tried to use my winter magic in the middle of an actual snowstorm before. But, Diary, there is a first time for everything.

I held my hands out while the cold wind blasted my face. I took a deep breath and focused. An ice column began

to rise from the ground. Up, up it climbed, like a skyscraper. Claudia stood by, tossing handfuls of glitter onto it.

By the time we finished, the ice column was so tall I couldn't see the top. We got in position for the next step.

I held the mixing bowl at the base of the column while Claudia operated the flashlight. We decided to flash the SOS signal, which means "We need help!" It goes like this:

S-three short flashes

O-three long flashes

S-three short flashes

The blizzard swirled all around us while Claudia flashed the signal again and again. Every time she flashed the light, my ice column lit up all sparkly (the glitter definitely helped). It was a beautiful distress call, but we had no idea whether it was really going to work.

Gusty barked and ran in circles

around the column of ice. "I know you want to help, buddy, but unless you can operate a flashlight, you're going to need to be quiet."

But Gusty would not stop barking into the storm.

"What's gotten into him?" asked Claudia.

"I have no idea! Gusty, calm down. It's just a light!"

That's when we heard it. Voices.

Was the storm playing tricks on our ears?

And then I heard someone far away calling, "Hello? Hello?"

I bent down to Gusty. "I know I just told you to be quiet, Gusty, but I need you to make a lot of noise right now!"

Gusty threw his head back. Diary, my little pup howled like a wolf!

Through the storm, we saw flashlights. A group of people came toward us. That's when I saw a face that made me literally jump with joy.

"Dad!"

18

My Really Great Great-Aunt

Dad was shocked to find out that the SOS signal he and the other pilots had been following led him to Claudia and me. We were the last people he expected to find on the ground during the snowstorm.

We followed him back to the airfield with the other pilots who had come out to look for us. They gave us blankets and hot chocolate. Gusty got water and some really good ear scratches.

Claudia and I thanked each pilot for coming out in the storm to find us. And

then Claudia got to call her parents and talk to them for a long time. I could tell she felt so much happier after hearing their voices.

"Dad?" I asked. "I'm going to be in the biggest trouble of my life when we get home, aren't I?"

He crossed his arms, then hugged me. "Maybe. But for now we can't even get home. The weather report says this storm is going to last for days."

"Are you sure about that?" asked one of the pilots, who was looking out the window. "Because the snow just stopped and the sun is coming out!"

We all ran to the window, amazed. How could a huge blizzard all of a sudden just stop?

Dad tapped my shoulder and pointed up to the sky. "I think somebody must have noticed you were missing."

If you didn't know what to look for, Diary, you would have thought it was a bird. But I knew exactly who it was.

Great-Aunt Eastia swooped through the clouds, her coat flapping out behind her. She was using her Windtamer powers to warm the air and blow the blizzard away. I knew she hated being in the cold, so I appreciated her even more.

In that moment, I was really proud of my great-aunt. I hoped that when she found out what Claudia and I did, she'd be proud of me too.

19

An Almost-Perfect Sleepover

So, Diary, that was the end of our big adventure with the blizzard. Well, almost the end.

After Great-Aunt Eastia cleared all the snow away, Dad flew me, Claudia, and Gusty back to the palace in his plane. When Mom opened the castle doors, she gave me a big, tight hug. And then she said, "Lina, you are in the biggest trouble of your life."

To my surprise, it was Great-Aunt Eastia who saved me.

"How can you talk about punishment when these poor, precious girls have been lost in the snow?" she cooed. She put her arms around me and Claudia and squeezed us until we couldn't breathe. "We can scold them later. Now is the time to spoil them rotten! So what do you girls want? Pizza? Hot dogs? You want to stay up late and

skate all over the castle? Your great-aunt Eastia is going to treat you like little princesses!"

"Actually," I said, rubbing my arms, "I would love some of your hot turnip soup if you have any left."

Claudia nodded. “And all I want to do is crawl into bed and go straight to sleep.”

And, Diary, that is pretty much what we did!

Make an Ice Lantern

Can you make a tower of ice light up, just like Lina and Claudia?

YOU WILL NEED:

- A medium or large plastic cup
- Small battery-powered votive "candle"
- Food coloring, glitter, sequins (totally optional, but fun!)

MIX AND FORM THE ICE LANTERN:

Fill your cup with water. If you want to, add food coloring or glitter and stir into the water. Put the cup into the freezer.

After about 1 to 2 hours, check on your cup. The water that is closest to the cold freezer air will begin freezing first, so ice will begin forming in the cup from the outside in. Take your cup out of the freezer when about a ¼- to ½-inch wall of ice has formed around the edges of the cup, but before the entire cup of water freezes solid. The freezing time will depend on the size of your cup and the temperature of your freezer, so you may have to keep checking on it!

When your ice has formed a frozen wall, take the cup out of the freezer. Gently tap on the surface of the ice to break a hole as wide as your votive. The water in the center of the cup should still be liquid. Pour it out. You will be left with a hollow shell of ice. Run the outside of the cup under warm water until the ice lantern slides out easily.

LIGHT IT UP:

Place your votive on a small plate and turn it on. Carefully set your ice lantern over the votive. Turn off the lights in the room. Now revel in your lantern's frozen beauty!

Some of the light from the votive will shine through the ice, out into the dark room. Some of the light will be reflected inside the ice lantern, causing it to glow. If Gusty were with you, he would howl with delight!

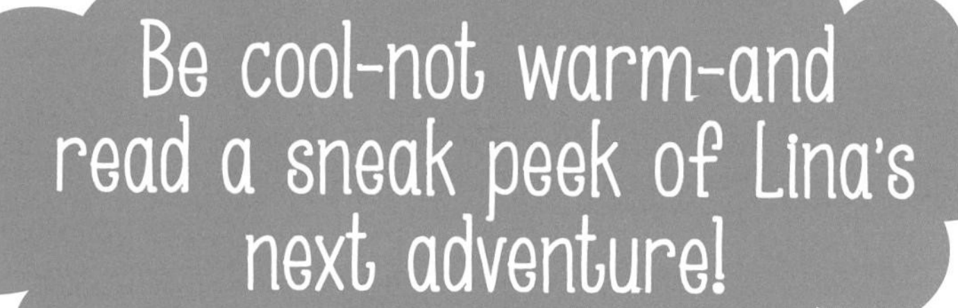
Be cool-not warm-and
read a sneak peek of Lina's
next adventure!

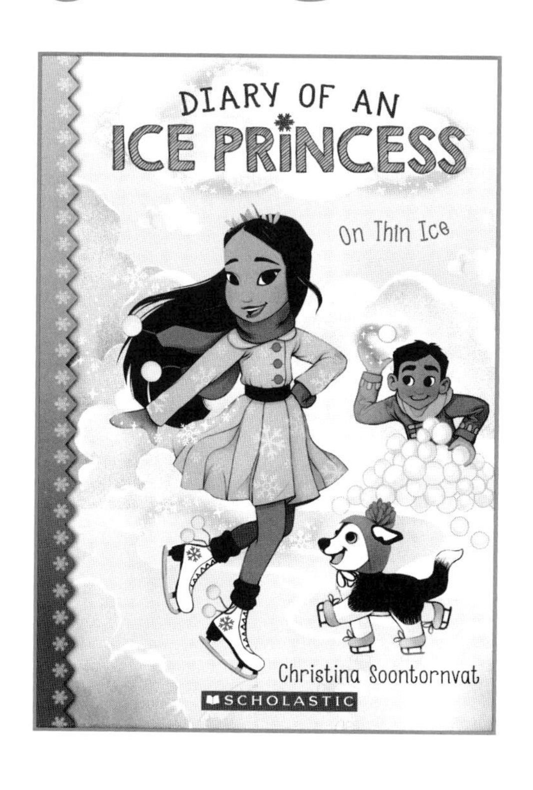
DIARY OF AN
ICE PRINCESS
On Thin Ice
Christina Soontornvat
SCHOLASTIC

1

THE TRUTH ABOUT FIELD TRIPS

FRIDAY

Diary, I am so excited!

Next week our class is going to do something called a *field trip*. When our teacher, Ms. Collier, first talked about it, I thought she meant we would take a trip to a field. We don't have fields up here in the clouds, so I thought it sounded fun.

I was even more excited when my best friend, Claudia, explained things.

"A field trip is when you get to go somewhere outside school," she said. "We all pack bag lunches, and the school bus will pick us up and take us somewhere cool."

I gasped with excitement. "Like the post office?"

Claudia laughed. "Even cooler than that. This year, our class is visiting Oceanside Aquarium."

An aquarium! I love watching animals that live underwater. Diary, I'm sure you remember the disaster that happened when I tried to set up an aquarium in my room.

Luckily, we hadn't bought any fish yet. That was back when my winter magic used to slip out without my control. I know for sure nothing like that would happen again.

This field trip is going to be so cool. I wish we could go tomorrow. But tomorrow is Saturday, which means the only trip I'll be taking is to Granddad's castle.

Saturdays are for Winterheart practice.

2

FAMILY NEWS

SATURDAY

I used to hate coming to Granddad's castle on Saturday mornings. But that was before I learned I was a Winterheart. Mom and Granddad are both Windtamers, which means they can control the wind and weather. I always thought I was a Windtamer too, but it turns out there are different types of magic in our family.

Once I figured out that my magic is all about snow and ice, practice with Granddad got a lot more fun.

This morning, he led me out to the fountain in his castle courtyard. **"ALL RIGHT, LINA, HAVE YOU BEEN PRACTICING?"**

(My granddad is the North Wind, and he yells a lot. You get used to it.)

I nodded and pushed up my sleeves. I let my breath out slowly and spread my fingers wide. The spray of water froze in midair, making a sheet of ice that looked just like glass. I felt pretty proud of myself.

Granddad raised one bushy eyebrow.

"THE ASSIGNMENT WAS TO FREEZE A SINGLE SPRAY OF WATER DROPLETS. NOT THE ENTIRE FOUNTAIN."

"Oh. But isn't it better to do things big?"

"NOT NECESSARILY. IT'S IMPORTANT FOR YOU TO LEARN HOW TO USE YOUR MAGIC IN SUBTLE WAYS TOO."

I frowned. This was coming from a guy who created the jet streams. Since when did Granddad ever do anything subtle?

Mom walked in with Gusty jumping at her feet.

"AH, GALE, THERE'S SOMETHING I WANTED TO TALK TO YOU ABOUT. DID YOU KNOW THAT LITTLE JACK IS

COMING UP FOR A VISIT FROM THE SOUTHERN HEMISPHERE?"

A half-sad, half-happy look flashed on Mom's face. "Is he really? We haven't seen him in years."

My cousin Jack lives with my great-aunt Sunder way down at the bottom of the globe, near Antarctica. My great-aunt Sunder is Granddad's sister, but she never comes to our family gatherings. I don't think they get along.

"HE WAS SUPPOSED TO STAY WITH ME," said Granddad. **"BUT PERHAPS HE COULD STAY WITH YOU INSTEAD. HE COULD GIVE LINA SOME LESSONS, WINTERHEART TO WINTERHEART."**

CHRISTINA SOONTORNVAT grew up behind the counter of her parents' Thai restaurant, reading stories. These days she loves to make up her own, especially if they involve magic. Christina also loves science and worked in a science museum for years before pursuing her dream of being an author. She still enjoys cooking up science experiments at home with her two young daughters. You can learn more about Christina and her books on her website at soontornvat.com.

Oh my glaciers, Diary!

Princess Lina is the *coolest* girl in school!

scholastic.com